CLASS   BOOK

UTICA PUBLIC LIBRARY
CHILDREN'S ROOM

OUR GALAXY AND BEYOND

PLUTO

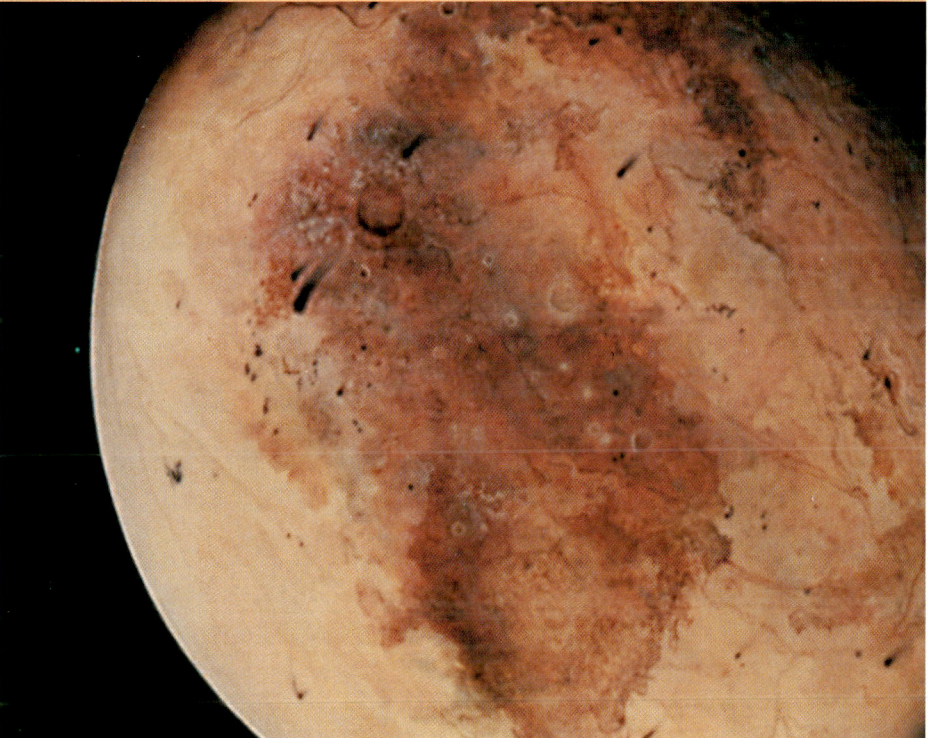

By Darlene R. Stille

THE CHILD'S WORLD®
CHANHASSEN, MINNESOTA

Published in the United States of America by The Child's World®
P.O. Box 326, Chanhassen, MN 55317-0326
800-599-READ
www.childsworld.com

*Content Adviser:
Michelle Nichols,
Lead Educator for
Informal Programs,
Adler Planetarium
& Astronomy
Museum, Chicago,
Illinois*

Photo Credits: Cover: NASA; Alan Fitzsimmons, Queens University, Belfast: 24; Bettmann/Corbis: 5, 7, 23; Corbis: 6 (Ali Meyer), 12, 14, 17 (Hubert Stadler), 18, 19, 25; Design Lab/ Kathy Petelinsek: 9; JHUAPL/SwRI: 27; NASA: 10 (HST/A. Field, STScI), 11 (HST), 21 (MODIS/Greg Bacon/STScI), 22 (A. Cochran, University of Texas); NASA/JPL/Caltech: 13 (2MASS), 16 (ESA/Alan Stern, SwRI/Marc Buie, Lowell Observatory); PS/CBAT/MPC/ICQ: 8; Roger Ressmeyer/Corbis: 4, 15 (NASA).

The Child's World®: Mary Berendes, Publishing Director
Editorial Directions, Inc.: E. Russell Primm, Editorial Director; Dana Rau, Line Editor; Elizabeth K. Martin, Assistant Editor; Olivia Nellums, Editorial Assistant; Susan Hindman, Copy Editor; Susan Ashley, Proofreader; Kevin Cunningham, Peter Garnham, Chris Simms, Fact Checkers; Tim Griffin/IndexServ, Indexer; Cian Loughlin O'Day, Photo Researcher; Linda S. Koutris, Photo Selector

Copyright © 2004 by The Child's World®
All rights reserved. No part of this book may be reproduced or utilized in any form or by any means without written permission from the publisher.

Library of Congress Cataloging-in-Publication Data
Stille, Darlene R.
  Pluto / by Darlene Stille.
     p. cm. — (Our galaxy and beyond)
Includes index.
Contents: Discovering Pluto—Pluto's atmosphere—What is Pluto made of?—Charon: moon or sister planet?—Beyond Pluto—How did Pluto form?
  ISBN 1-59296-053-7 (lib. bdg. : alk. paper)
1. Pluto (Planet)—Juvenile literature. [1. Pluto (Planet)] I. Title. II. Series.
QB701.S85 2004
523.48'2—dc21   2003008039

Table of Contents

CHAPTER ONE
4 Discovering Pluto

CHAPTER TWO
13 Pluto's Atmosphere

CHAPTER THREE
15 What Pluto Is Made Of

CHAPTER FOUR
18 Charon: Moon or Sister Planet?

CHAPTER FIVE
22 Beyond Pluto

CHAPTER SIX
26 How Pluto May Have Formed

28 Glossary

28 Did You Know?

29 Fast Facts

30 How to Learn More about Pluto

32 Index

CHAPTER ONE

Discovering Pluto

A young **astronomer** studied his pictures carefully. He had taken the pictures with a camera on a powerful **telescope** at the Lowell **Observatory** near Flagstaff, Arizona. The pictures were on special glass plates. The astronomer, Clyde Tombaugh, compared one picture with another. He was looking for Planet X.

Pluto was first seen through the Clark Telescope at the Lowell Observatory in Flagstaff, Arizona.

Many years before, another astronomer had noticed that the planet Neptune moved strangely as it orbited, or went around, the Sun. He thought that a ninth planet in our solar system beyond Neptune would explain those movements. He called the unknown planet Planet X. He used math to figure out where Planet X should be in the sky. The man who came up with the Planet X idea was a famous astronomer named Percival Lowell. He was very rich and was able to build his own observatory. Lowell started to search for Planet X, but he died in 1916 before he could find it.

Percival Lowell thought the strange movements of Neptune indicated another planet beyond it. He turned out to be right.

No one else looked for Planet X until Clyde Tombaugh came to the Lowell Observatory in 1929. Tombaugh used a new, more powerful telescope to take pictures of the sky. At first, he just saw hundreds of distant stars that looked like dots. One day, he spotted a difference in the pictures. One of the dots had moved! In March 1930, he announced that the dot was Planet X. This discovery made Clyde Tombaugh famous. The newly discovered planet was named Pluto, after the ancient Roman god of the underworld. All of the planets, except Earth and Uranus, are named after Roman gods or goddesses.

People have been naming things (including objects in our solar system) after the Roman gods and goddesses for hundreds of years. Here they are seen at a banquet in a painting from the 1600s.

CLYDE TOMBAUGH

As a boy, Clyde William Tombaugh (with telescope below) loved to look at the sky. He even made his own telescopes. Tombaugh was born in the town of Streator, Illinois, in 1906. Later, his family moved to a farm in western Kansas. The Kansas countryside was very dark at night because there were no city lights. Dark nights are good for viewing stars and planets.

In 1929, he was invited to work at the Lowell Observatory. Clyde took a train to Flagstaff, Arizona. He was a little scared and lonely. He had no money, and he was a long way from his Kansas home. He slept in a room at the observatory. He spent many chilly nights taking pictures with the observatory's big telescope. He worked hard studying pictures of the sky.

Tombaugh continued working at the Lowell Observatory for the next 13 years. He is most famous for discovering Pluto, but over the years, he also found a **comet,** many **asteroids,** clusters of stars, and many groups of stars called galaxies. He died in New Mexico in 1997, just before his 91st birthday.

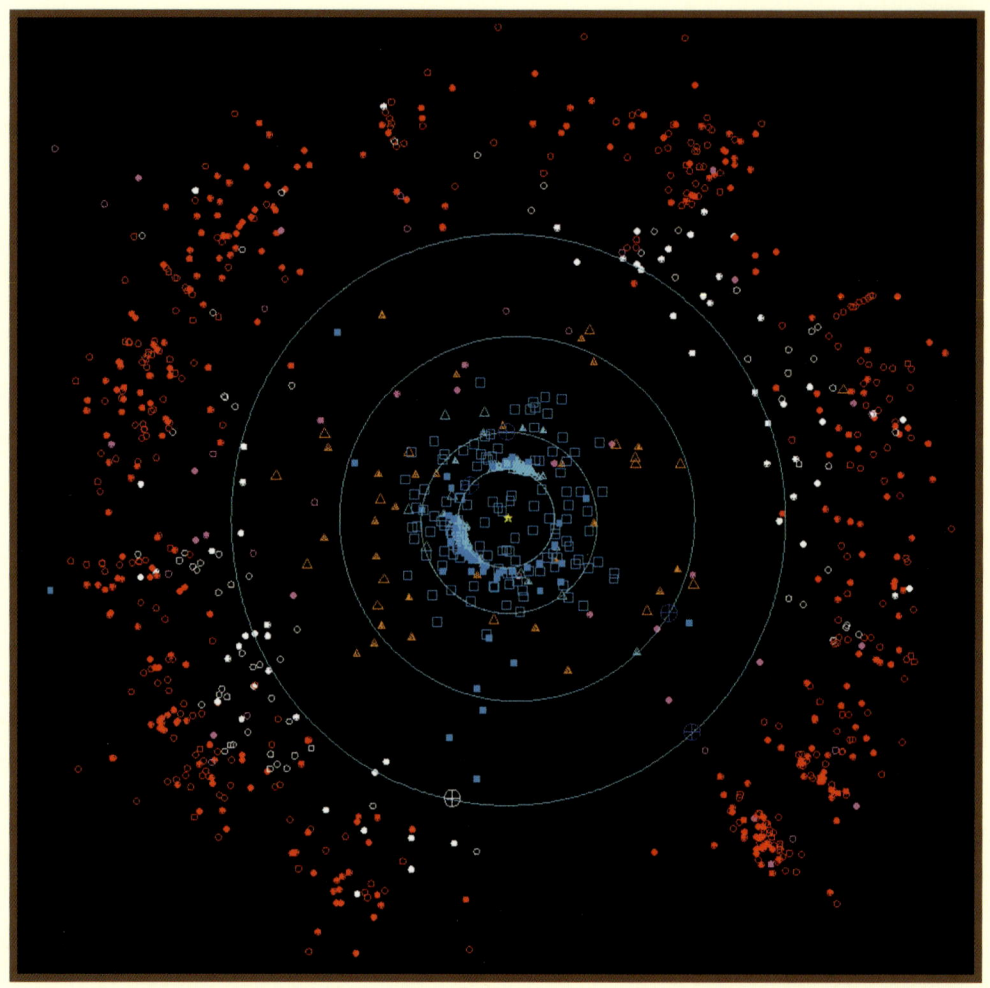

In this scientific drawing, the turquoise rings represent the orbits of four of the outer planets. From the center outward they are Jupiter, Saturn, Uranus, and Neptune. If Pluto's orbit were shown on this picture, it would be a long oval shape that crossed over the orbit line of Neptune.

Like the other planets, Pluto orbits the Sun. It takes Pluto 248 Earth-years to go around the Sun once. Pluto's path around the Sun is shaped like a long oval. Sometimes Pluto's orbit takes it closer to the Sun. Sometimes its orbit takes it far away. The closest Pluto ever gets to the Sun is about 2.8 billion miles (4.5 billion kilometers). This tiny planet is an average of 3.7 billion miles (5.9 billion km) from the Sun.

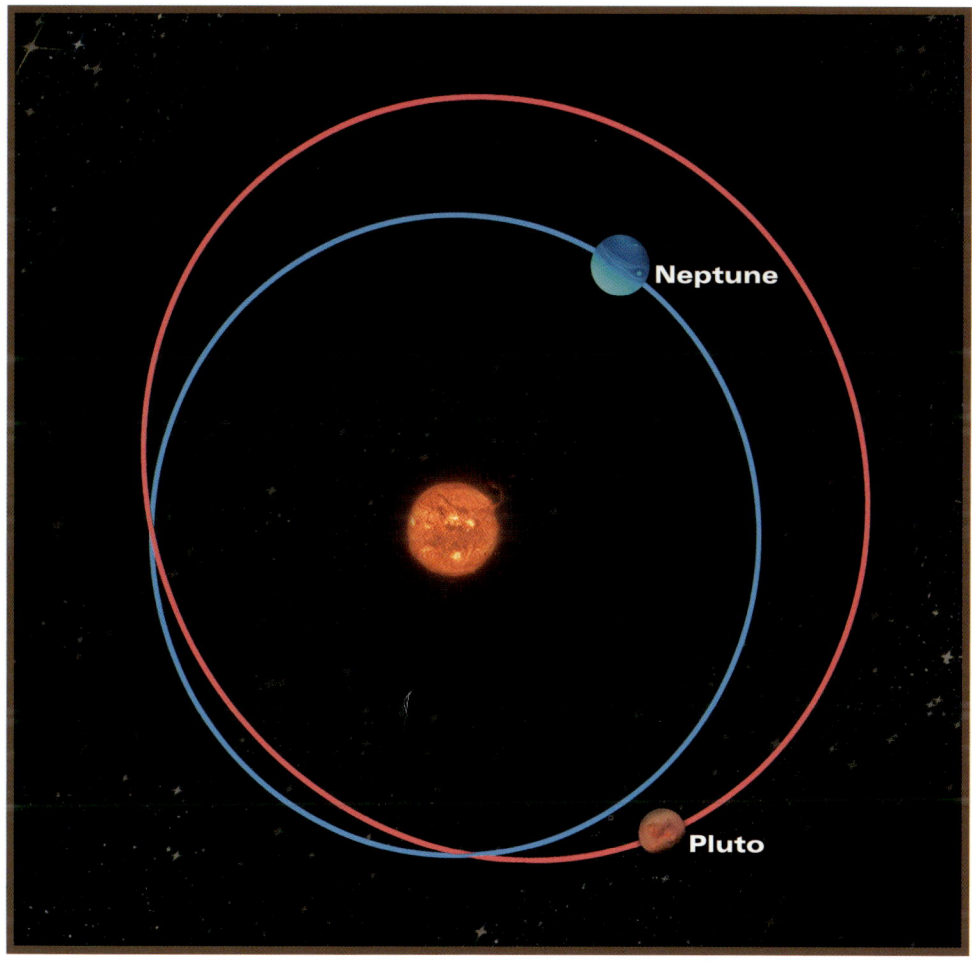

Pluto's orbit is oval shaped and crosses the orbit of Neptune. For certain periods of time, Pluto is the eighth planet from the Sun and Neptune is the ninth.

Even though scientists aren't sure of Pluto's exact diameter, this diagram shows how small its diameter might be compared to Earth and Earth's Moon. Pluto is so far from Earth that trying to see its surface in detail is like trying to read the printing on a golf ball from 33 miles (54 km) away.

Pluto is the smallest planet in our solar system. It is less than one-fifth the size of Earth. It is even smaller than Earth's Moon. But Pluto is so far away that scientists are not sure about its exact size. They think it has a **diameter** of about 1,430 miles (2,300 km). That is less than the distance from Chicago to San Francisco. This may seem like a long way on Earth. But imagine trying to see something that size from billions of miles away. No wonder it was so hard to find Pluto!

Pluto is the farthest planet from the Sun. But for a 20-year period, Pluto comes closer to the Sun than Neptune, the eighth planet. That 20-year period happens once every 228 years. From January 23, 1979, until February 11, 1999, Pluto was closer to

From Pluto, the Sun would look no brighter than this star does from Earth.

the Sun than Neptune. Pluto will not come this close again until the 2200s.

No spacecraft has ever visited Pluto to take close-up pictures. Robot spacecraft have visited every other planet. Astronomers have had to use telescopes to study Pluto. They use powerful telescopes on Earth. They have also learned much about Pluto by studying pictures and measurements made by the Hubble Space Telescope and other telescopes that orbit above Earth. Most of what we know about Pluto we have learned since the 1970s because of these new, powerful telescopes.

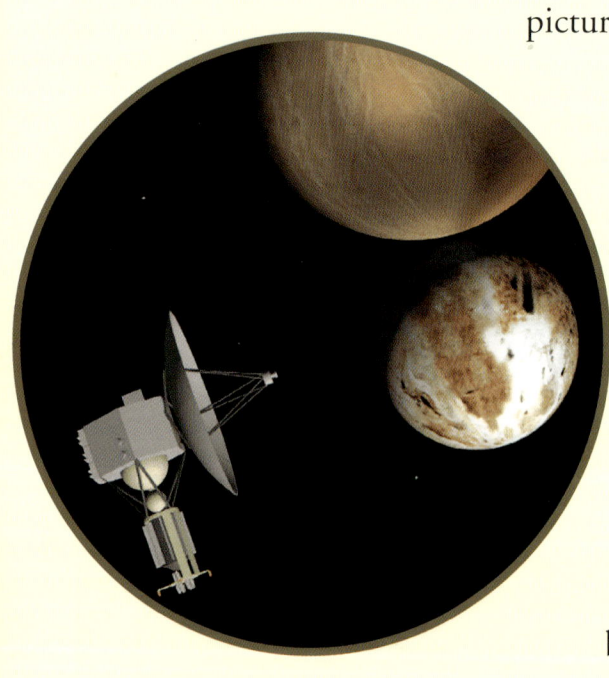

Although no spacecraft have visited Pluto yet, artists present their ideas of what such a voyage might be like.

CHAPTER TWO

Pluto's Atmosphere

Sometimes Pluto has an atmosphere, and sometimes it doesn't. An atmosphere is the layer of gases that surrounds a planet. When Pluto is far from the Sun, it is too cold to have an atmosphere. Pluto is one of the coldest places in the solar system. Temperatures may drop as low as –387° Fahrenheit (–233° Celsius) or even colder. The gases in Pluto's atmosphere freeze when it gets this cold, the way that

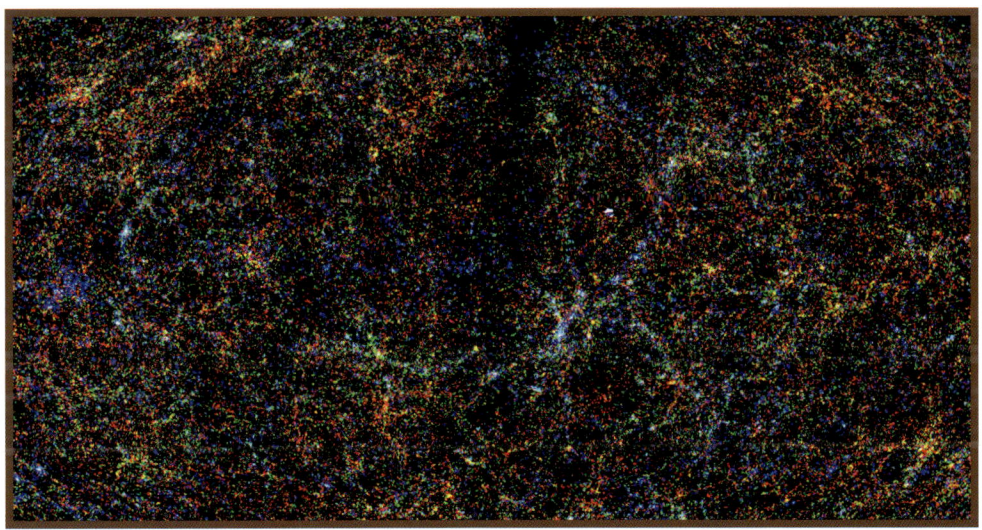

Pluto rotates so far from the sun that its warmest temperatures are far below the coldest temperatures on Earth. In this wide view of the sky, our solar system is just a speck somewhere in the darker band at the center. The parts of the universe closest to Earth show up as blue here and the farthest away are red.

the steam made from water can freeze into ice. When Pluto gets closer to the Sun, the Sun's heat warms the planet's surface. The ice changes back into gases to form an atmosphere.

When Pluto is close to the Sun, it has a thin atmosphere. A thin atmosphere is one that does not have a lot of gas in it. Astronomers think that Pluto's atmosphere is made up mostly of a gas called nitrogen. This is the gas that makes up most of Earth's atmosphere. Pluto's atmosphere also has some gases called methane and carbon monoxide. Carbon monoxide is poisonous to human beings.

The gases that make up Earth's atmosphere keep the weather lively and changing all the time. Here Hurricane Gladys can be seen from space.

CHAPTER THREE

What Pluto Is Made Of

Even powerful telescopes on Earth cannot clearly see the surface of Pluto. Pluto usually looks like a bright blob in pictures taken by most telescopes. In 1994, astronomers saw good pictures of Pluto's surface for the first time. These pictures were taken by the Hubble Space Telescope.

The pictures show very bright areas and very dark areas on Pluto's surface. Hubble found 12 of these areas. What could cause such bright or dark patches? The bright areas may be frozen nitrogen. The dark areas may be

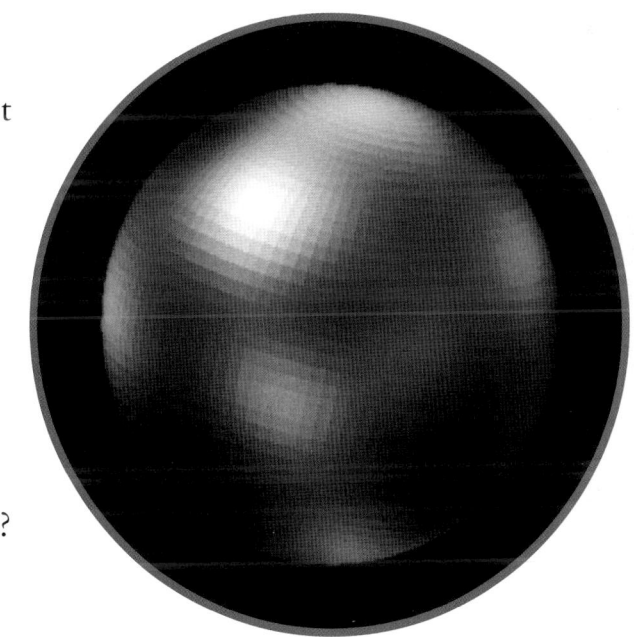

This picture, taken from space by the Hubble Space Telescope, shows the dark and bright areas on Pluto's surface. But no one understands yet what they are or what causes them.

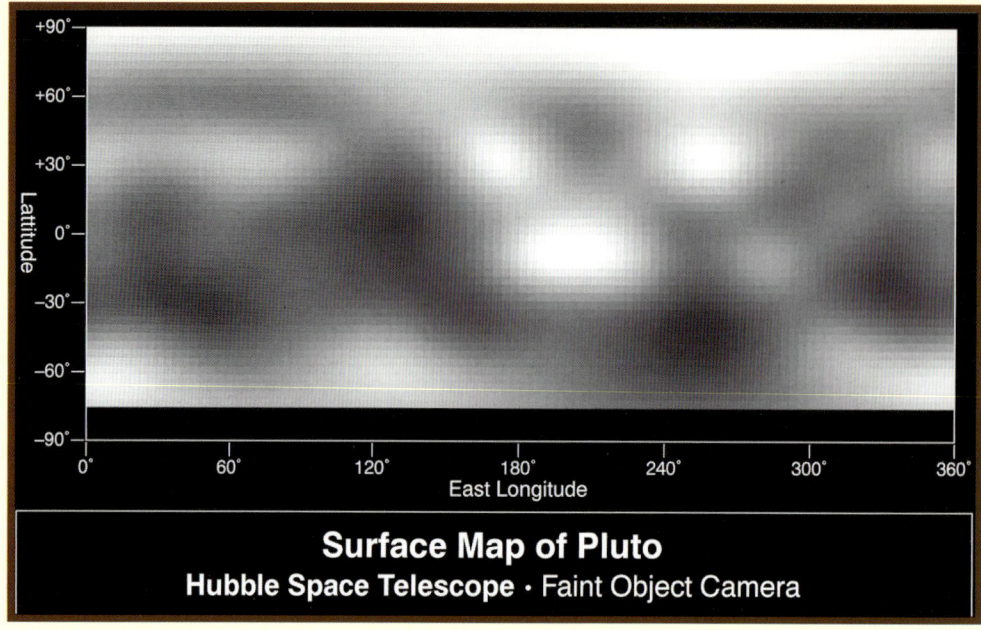

A powerful computer was able to put together this image of Pluto's surface from four pictures taken of its surface while it rotated. Though the image is blurry, scientists know that the poles of the planet are lighter in color and that there is a dark belt around its equator. But is it really a planet?

frozen methane. Some of the bright or dark areas may be caused by craters or ridges on the planet. Craters are large holes on the surface of a planet or a moon. They are created when a comet or **meteorite** crashes into the surface.

Scientists can only guess what Pluto is made of. They think there may be rock and frozen water under Pluto's surface. Pluto may have a center, or core, made of solid rock. Maybe there are layers of frozen water around the rocky core. Maybe the icy layers inside Pluto move around. Heat deep inside the planet could make the ice move like ice crushed in a blender. Many planets, including Earth, are hot inside. Scientists will have to keep guessing what Pluto is like until a spacecraft gets a closer look at the planet.

This cold, icy scene on Earth would seem as hot as the hottest summer day compared to the temperatures on Pluto. Scientists think there may be layers of ice beneath Pluto's surface and possibly frozen gases above.

CHAPTER FOUR

Charon: Moon or Sister Planet?

Pluto has one moon. A moon is a natural object that orbits a planet. Pluto's moon is very unusual. It was discovered in 1978 and named Charon. Charon has a diameter of about 790 miles

Pluto (above and larger) and Charon are still mysterious. But scientists hope to find out much more about them in the coming years.

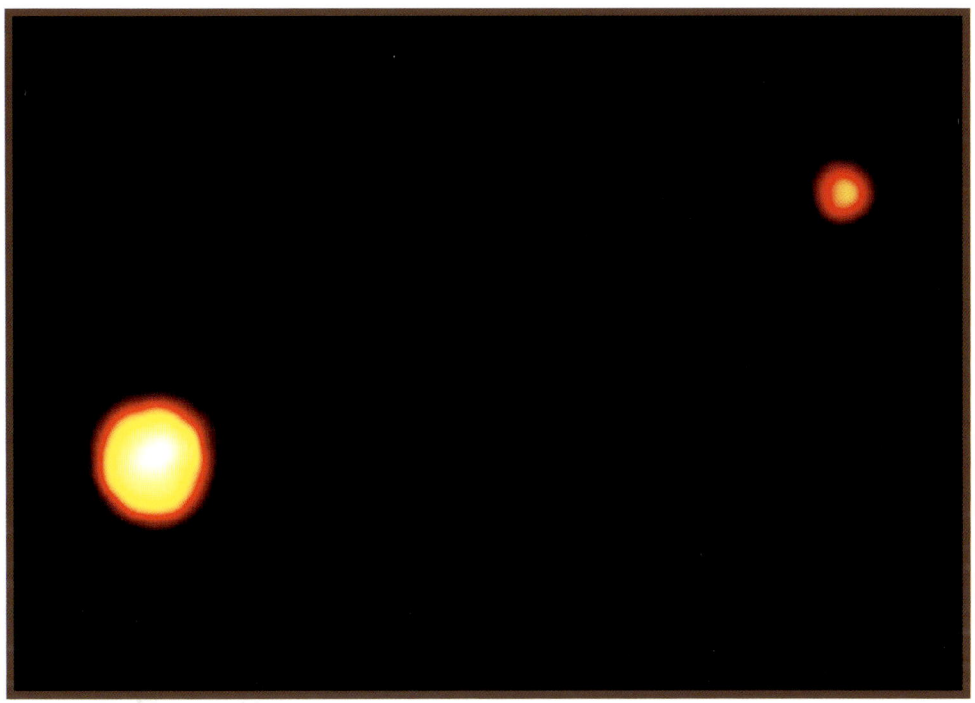

Pluto and Charon dance around each other at the far end of the solar system. Because of their different colors, scientists feel certain their surfaces are made of different substances.

(1,270 km). It is about half the size of Pluto. This is very big for a moon, especially for a planet so small. Charon is also very close to Pluto. It is less than 12,000 miles (19,300 km) away. Our Moon is 238, 857 miles (384,403 km) from Earth.

Because it is so close, Charon does not go around Pluto the way our Moon orbits Earth. Instead, Pluto and Charon orbit each other.

They are like two dancers twirling around a point between them. Astronomers wonder whether Pluto and Charon are a double planet, rather than a planet and a moon.

Charon may once have been part of Pluto. A comet or other large object could have crashed into Pluto and sent pieces of the planet into space. The pieces might have come together to form a moon. Some scientists think this is how Earth's Moon may also have formed.

Pluto and Charon seem to have different kinds of surfaces. Charon has a darker surface. It does not reflect as much of the Sun's light as Pluto. This may be a sign that the surface of Charon is covered with dirty ice made of water. The ice on Pluto's surface may be mainly frozen nitrogen, not frozen water. Why their surfaces are so different is a mystery.

QUAOAR: THE NEWEST SOLAR SYSTEM DISCOVERY

Astronomers at the California Institute of Technology found a new, icy world beyond Pluto in 2002. It was the biggest object found in the solar system since the discovery of Pluto. The astronomers named it Quaoar (pronounced KWAH-o-whar) after a god that Native Americans believe created Earth.

The astronomers found Quaoar when they were looking through a telescope on Earth. Then the Hubble Space Telescope took pictures of Quaoar. It seems to be like a comet. It is probably made of rock and ice. But it is much bigger than a comet. Quaoar's diameter is about 800 miles (1,300 km). It is about half the size of Pluto. Below, scientists placed an artist's representation of Quaoar over a satellite photograph of North America. This gives you a good understanding of how small Quaoar is.

CHAPTER FIVE

Beyond Pluto

Pluto is far out in the solar system, but it has lots of company. Pluto lies in a zone of icy balls beyond the orbit of Neptune. This zone is called the Kuiper (KYE-pur) Belt. The icy balls are called Kuiper Belt Objects (KBOs).

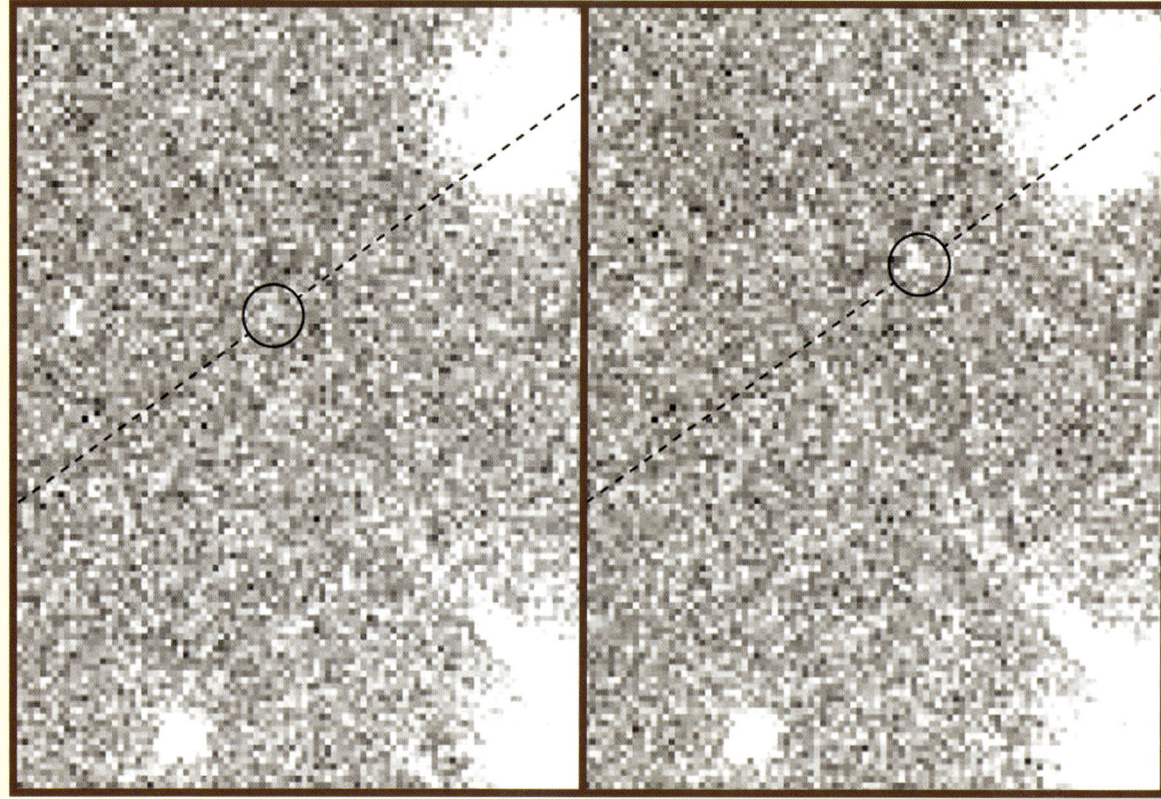

Scientists at NASA look at strange photos like these of Kuiper Belt Objects to understand what is going on in the region around Pluto.

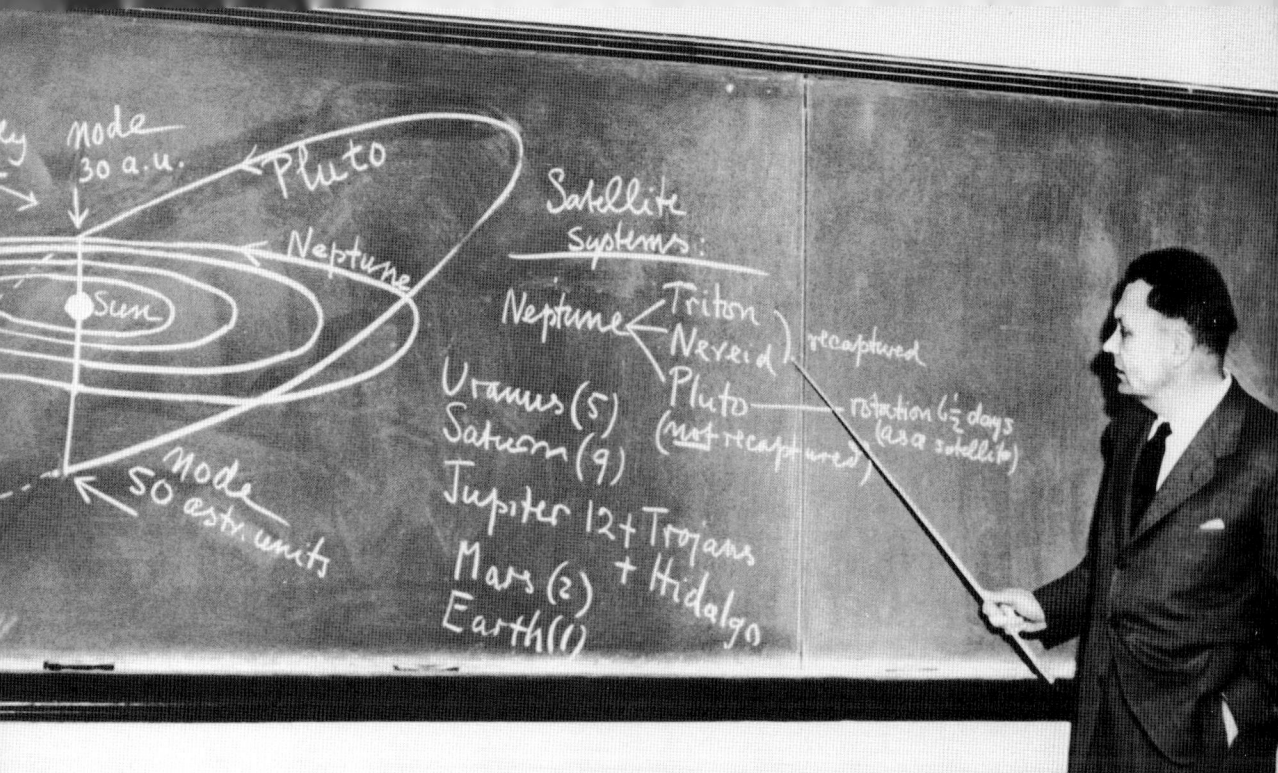

As Dr. Kuiper points out here at the blackboard, Neptune usually orbits closer to the Sun than Pluto does. But because of its unusual orbit, every 228 years Pluto is the one that rotates closer to the Sun.

The Kuiper Belt is named for the astronomer Gerard Kuiper. In the 1950s, he came up with a new idea about the solar system. He thought that there might be some chunks left from when the solar system formed. Astronomers think the planets formed about 4.6 billion years ago from a hot, swirling cloud of gas and dust around the Sun. Some material never came together to form planets. Kuiper thought the chunks of leftover dust and gas might be in an area beyond

Neptune. Some astronomers call the Kuiper Belt the solar system's final **frontier,** because it is so far from the Sun.

In the 1990s, astronomers began finding KBOs. They think the Kuiper Belt contains at least 70,000 KBOs circling the Sun. After they found the Kuiper Belt, some astronomers began to wonder whether Pluto is a planet. They think it may just be the biggest KBO yet found.

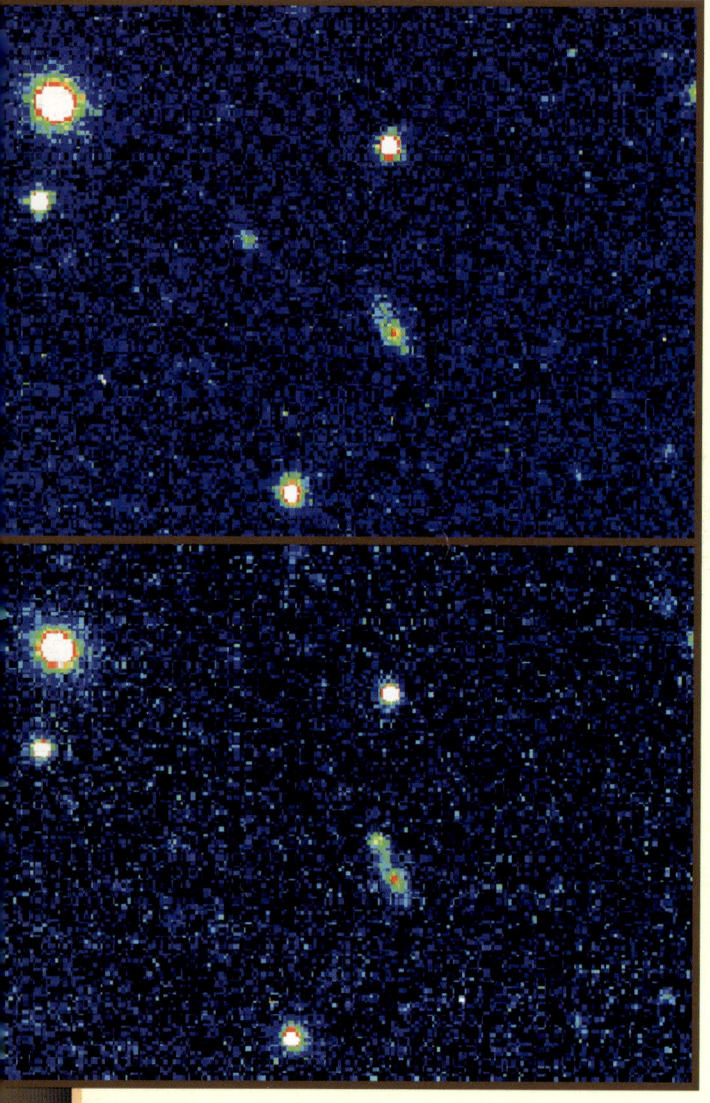

These two photos show one of the brightest Kuiper Belt Objects scientists have found so far. One photo was taken a little less than five hours after the other. From these pictures scientists were able to determine that the object was farther away than Neptune but still inside our solar system.

IS PLUTO A PLANET?

Some astronomers do not think Pluto is a planet. These astronomers say that Pluto does not look like its four nearest neighbor planets. Jupiter, Saturn, Uranus, and Neptune are all huge balls of gas. Pluto is a small ball of ice. Also, Pluto is in a zone of the solar system called the Kuiper Belt. Objects in this belt are all small and icy. So some astronomers think that Pluto is just a big Kuiper Belt Object.

Other astronomers think Pluto really is a planet. They say that a planet is an object that is round like a ball and orbits the Sun. Pluto fits this definition. These astronomers think there may be more small planets beyond Pluto.

What do you think?

CHAPTER SIX

How Pluto May Have Formed

The early solar system was made from a cloud of dust and gas. This cloud became the Sun and the planets. Over billions of years, the planets have changed. It is hard to tell from studying the planets today what the early solar system was like. But Pluto and other KBOs might still have material from the time the planets formed.

This is because the Kuiper Belt is very cold. The original gas and dust from the beginning of the solar system may be frozen inside KBOs. Pluto may have these materials frozen inside as well.

The best way to learn more about Pluto is to send a robot spacecraft there. In the early 2000s, the National Aeronautics and Space Administration (NASA) was making plans to do that. They named the mission New Horizons. They plan to launch a spacecraft in 2006 or

2007. The spacecraft will visit Pluto around 2015. It will then go on to explore the Kuiper Belt.

Meanwhile, astronomers use all kinds of telescopes to study Pluto and look for more KBOs. They believe these distant, icy objects can tell us much about our solar system and how it came to be.

An artist's drawing of the spacecraft that will investigate Pluto and the regions around it in 2015 as part of the New Horizons mission.

Glossary

asteroids (ASS-tuh-royds) Asteroids are rocky objects that orbit the Sun.

astronomer (uh-STRAW-nuh-mer) An astronomer is a scientist who studies space and the stars and planets.

comet (KOM-it) A comet is a bright object, followed by a tail of dust and ice, that orbits the Sun in a long, oval-shaped path.

diameter (dye-AM-uh-tuhr) A planet's diameter is the length of a straight line going through the center of it, from one side to the other.

frontier (fruhn-TIHR) A frontier is the outer edge of a place or a country.

meteorite (MEE-tee-uh-rite) A meteorite is a rocky or metallic object from space that hits the surface of a planet or moon.

observatory (uhb-ZUR-vuh-tor-ee) An observatory is a building in which scientists can study space and the stars and planets through telescopes and other instruments.

telescope (TEL-uh-skope) A telescope is an instrument used to study things that are far away, such as stars and planets, by making them seem larger and closer.

Did You Know?

▶ If you could stand on the surface of Pluto and look up at the sky, the Sun wouldn't look like a large yellow ball the way it does from Earth. It would just look like a small, bright star. The Sun would look so small because Pluto is an average of 3.7 billion miles (5.9 billion km) from the Sun.

▶ How hard is it to study Pluto? Imagine looking down a straight road that is 33 miles (53 km) long. At the end of the road, there is a golf ball with writing on it. Trying to see the surface of Pluto from Earth is like trying to read the writing on that golf ball.

- Something that makes Pluto different from most planets is that it rolls rather than spins. Every planet has an axis, an imaginary stick going down the middle from its top to its bottom. A planet is usually tipped on its axis. Pluto is so tipped that it looks like it is lying on its side as it goes around the Sun. Uranus also seems to roll on its axis.

- Before Charon was discovered in 1978, astronomers thought Pluto was much bigger than it really is. That is because they saw Pluto and its moon Charon blurred together.

Fast Facts

Diameter: about 1,430 miles (2,300 kilometers)

Atmosphere: nitrogen, methane, carbon monoxide

Time to orbit the Sun (one Pluto-year): 248 Earth-years

Time to turn on axis (one Pluto-day): 6.4 Earth-days

Shortest distance from Sun: 2.8 billion miles (4.4 billion km)

Greatest distance from Sun: 4.5 billion miles (7.4 billion km)

Shortest distance from Earth: 2.7 billion miles (4.3 billion km)

Greatest distance from Earth: 4.7 billion miles (7.5 billion km)

Average surface temperature: about −380° F (−229° C)

Surface gravity: 0.05 that of Earth. A person weighing 80 pounds (36 kg) on Earth would weigh 4 pounds (2 kg) on Pluto.

Number of known moons: 1

How to Learn More about Pluto

At the Library

Asimov, Isaac, and Richard Hantula. *Pluto and Charon.* Milwaukee: Gareth Stevens, 2002.

Brimner, Larry. *Pluto.* New York: Children's Press, 2001.

Goss, Tim. *Uranus, Neptune, and Pluto.* Chicago: Heinemann Library, 2003.

Nardo, Don. *Pluto.* San Diego: Kidhaven, 2003.

Stefoff, Rebecca. *Pluto.* New York: Benchmark Books, 2003.

Tocci, Salvatore. *A Look at Pluto.* New York: Franklin Watts, 2003.

On the Web

Visit our home page for lots of links about Pluto:
http://www.childsworld.com/links.html
Note to Parents, Teachers, and Librarians: We routinely verify our Web links to make sure they're safe, active sites—so encourage your readers to check them out!

Through the Mail or by Phone

ADLER PLANETARIUM AND ASTRONOMY MUSEUM
1300 South Lake Shore Drive
Chicago, IL 60605-2403
312/922-STAR

NATIONAL AIR AND SPACE MUSEUM
7th and Independence Avenue, S.W.
Washington, DC 20560
202/357-2700

ROSE CENTER FOR EARTH AND SPACE
AMERICAN MUSEUM OF NATURAL HISTORY
Central Park West at 79th Street
New York, NY 10024-5192
212/769-5100

The solar system

Index

astronomers, 4–5, 12, 14, 20, 21, 23, 24, 25
atmosphere, 13–14

California Institute of Technology, 21
carbon monoxide, 14
Charon, 18–20
core, 16–17
craters, 16

diameter, 10

formation, 23, 26

galaxies, 7

Hubble Space Telescope, 12, 15, 21

ice, 14, 17, 20, 25

Kuiper Belt, 22–24, 25, 26
Kuiper Belt Objects (KBOs), 22, 24, 25, 26, 27
Kuiper, Gerard, 23

Lowell Observatory, 4, 5, 7

Lowell, Percival, 5

methane, 14, 16
moon, 18–20

name, 6
National Aeronautics and Space Administration (NASA), 26
New Horizons mission, 26–27
nitrogen, 14, 15, 20

orbit, 8–9, 11–12, 19–20

Planet X, 4, 5, 6

Quaoar, 21

size, 10–11
solar system, 23, 24, 27
spacecraft, 12, 26–27
Sun, 5, 8–9, 11–12, 13, 14, 20, 23, 25, 26
surface, 14, 15, 20

telescopes, 4, 6, 7, 12, 15
temperatures, 13–14
Tombaugh, Clyde William, 4, 5–6, 7

About the Author

Darlene R. Stille is a science writer. She has lived in Chicago, Illinois, all her life. When she was in high school, she fell in love with science. While attending the University of Illinois she discovered that she also loved writing. She was fortunate to find a career that allowed her to combine both her interests. Darlene Stille has written about 60 books for young people.